Meet Kaliyah
KIND GIRL CROSSING
Jennifer A. Roberts

AuthorHouse™
1663 Liberty Drive
Bloomington, IN 47403
www.authorhouse.com
Phone: 1 (800) 839-8640

Published by AuthorHouse 08/22/2019

ISBN: 978-1-7283-0228-7 (sc)
ISBN: 978-1-7283-0229-4 (e)

Library of Congress Control Number: 2019902404

Print information available on the last page.

This book is printed on acid-free paper.

authorHOUSE®

Meet Kaliyah

Hi! I'm Kaliyah Richardson. I am six years old. My favorite colors are purple and pink. I have two favorite colors because I can't decide which one I like best. I love to read, draw flowers and play on the computer. I also like riding my bike, playing dress up and pretending to be a cashier. When I grow up I want to be a singer, salon owner and a pediatrician. That sounds like a lot but I can handle it!

I live with my daddy, mommy, little brother, Warren and our dog, Louie. I love my family because they love me. They teach me to be kind and responsible. My parents spend a lot of time with my brother and I playing games, attending church, and going on family field trips and vacations. Next summer we are going to Adventureland. I cant' wait!

I am Loved
I am Smart
I am The Best
1+1=2
2+2=4
1-"20
MATHMATICS
1+1=2
CONSTRUCTION VEHICLES

One of my favorite things to do is play school with Warren. Of course I am the teacher and he is the student. I teach him how to read books, count and write his letters. He's a very good student.

My daddy is the coolest! He is an entrepreneur. That is a grown-up word for someone who owns their own business. He works hard to make sure that our family has all the things we need like a nice house to live in, food to eat and clothes to wear. He also works hard so that we can buy things we want like lip gloss, ice cream and slime.

My mommy is the best! She is a stay at home mom which means that her job is to take care of Warren and I and make our home comfortable. She cooks great food, plays with me, reads to me, takes me places and cleans up after me. She also helps me with math. When I get hurt she always makes my "boo boos" feel better.

I love my little brother. He's three and he's so cute. He likes dinosaurs, trucks, books, blocks and climbing. He and I love to play tag but my Mom says that if we keep running through the house someone is going to get hurt. I think she's just making that up.

R

Louie is our family dog and he is awesome! We adopted him from the pet store last year around Christmas time. I still remember the night we brought him home. Warren and I were so excited because we really wanted a dog. I love to give Louie kisses and rub his soft fur. He likes when I play fetch with him outside and give him peanut butter treats.

Shape Posters
Circle
Square
Triangle
Hexagon
Pentagon
Diamond
Heart
When you see a
message from Miss M:
What are your HOPES for 1st grade?
PEGGY
LOKI
FRODO
JADE
TOTO

I am a first grader at Winchester Academy. I love school and have the best teacher, Mrs. Clemson. She makes the school day fun and exciting. On the first day of school Mrs. Clemson wore big, yellow sunglasses and a silly hat to class. She said she did that because she knew it would make her new students smile and feel more comfortable. She also greeted each student at the door and welcomed us by name. I still don't know how she knew everyone's name on the first day of school. Two weeks ago, we planted lima bean seeds in a cup. Every day we check on our plants and give them water if they are dry. I named my plant Peggy.

MONTHS
JANUARY
FEBRUARY
MARCH
APRIL
MAY
JUNE
JULY
AUGUST
SEPTEMBER
OCTOBER
NOVEMBER
DECEMBER
AUGUST
Days of the Week
SUNDAY
MONDAY
WEATHER
NUMBER CHART
Today's Date is
Monday, August 27th
SCHOOL BUS
SMART GIRLS ROCK
KIND IS COOL

My best friend, Madison and I are in the same class. We've been friends since we were in preschool. We have a lot in common. We are kind, smart, love playing with dolls and eating pizza. In class, we compete to see who can raise their hand the fastest when Mrs. Clemson asks a question. Madison and I sit together at lunch and play tag during recess.

ICED TEA
LEMONADE

After school I like to play with Warren, watch television or read. When the weather is nice Mommy takes us to the playground. My favorite time of the evening is dinner time. I love when my family sits around the table to discuss our day. I have a great family and a great life. It’s so much fun being me.

Printed in the United States
By Bookmasters

Hi! I'm Kaliyah Richardson and I am six years old. I live with my daddy, mommy, little brother, Warren and our dog, Louie. When I grow up, I want to be a singer, salon owner, and a pediatrician. That sounds like a lot but I can handle it!

authorHOUSE®

ISBN 978-1-7283-0228-7
9 781728 302287

A VIEW TO A DOOR

A Collection of Abstract Essays: A Book of Peace and Harmony

JANE SUMMERS